Birdie's Beauty Parlor

Lee Merrill Byrd

Illustrated by
Francisco Delgado

For Birdie, Citlali and Itzel

FIRST EDITION 10 9 8 7 6 5 4 3 2 1 Library of Congress Cataloging-in-Publication Data Names: Byrd, Lee Merrill, author. | Delgado, Francisco, 1974— illustrator. Title: Birdie's beauty parlor = El salón de belleza de Birdie / by Lee Merrill Byrd; illustrated by Francisco Delgado. Description: First edition. | El Paso, Texas : Cinco Puntos Press, [2020] |Identifiers: ISBN 978-1-947627-28-4 (cloth ; alk. paper) ISBN 978-1-947627-29-1 (e-book) Subjects: | CYAC: Beauty shops—Fiction. | Play—Fiction. | Grandmothers—Fiction. | Hispanic Americans—Fiction. | Spanish language materials—Bilingual. | BISAC: JUVENILE FICTION / Imagination & Play. | JUVENILE FICTION / Family /Multigenerational. | JUVENILE FICTION / Social Issues / Friendship. | JUVENILE FICTION / Girls & Women. Classification: LCC PZ73 (ebook) | LCC PZ73 .B93 2018 (print) | DDC [E]--dc23 LC record available at https://ccn.loc.gov/201704566

If your grandma looks tired, it means she needs a good beauty parlor.

Si tu abue se ve cansada, es hora de un buen salón de belleza.

Que se acueste en su cama,
encima de una toalla.

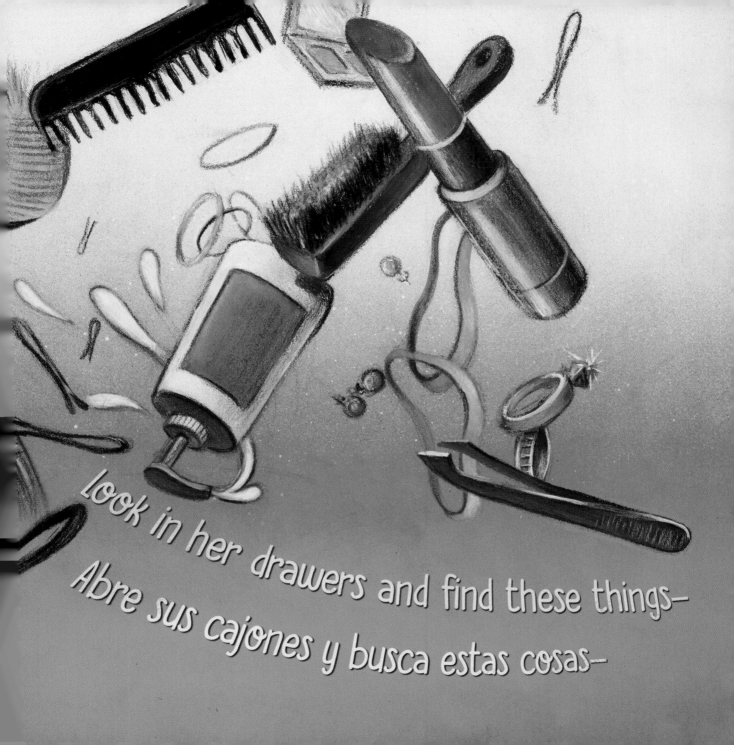

Look in her drawers and find these things—

Abre sus cajones y busca estas cosas—

Dump all the stuff on the bed.

Echa todo en la cama.

See if your grandma's chin has hairs on it.
Pull them out!
Ouch! Ouch!

Revisa la barbilla de tu abuela
para ver si tiene vellos.
¡Ay! ¡Ay!

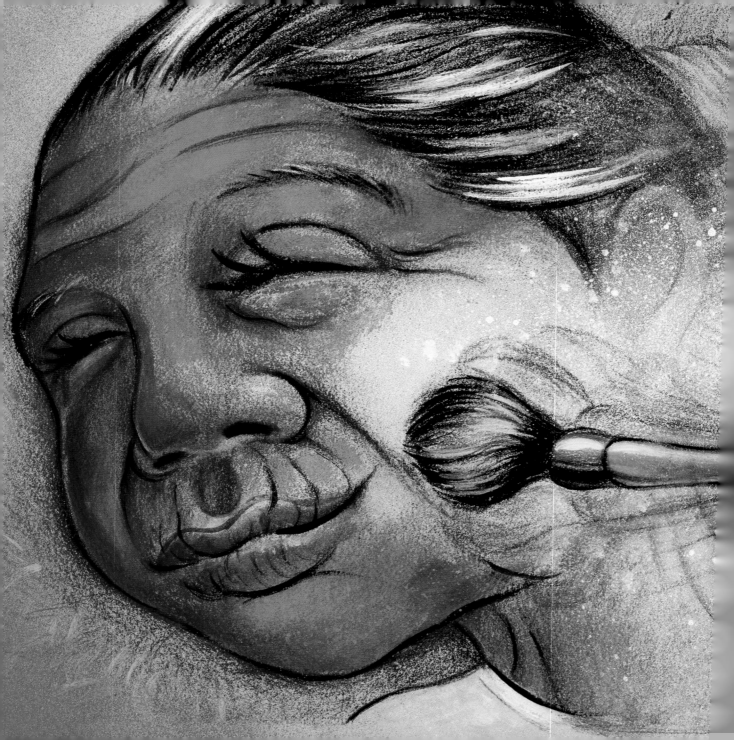

Put powder all over her face.

Ponle talco en toda la cara.

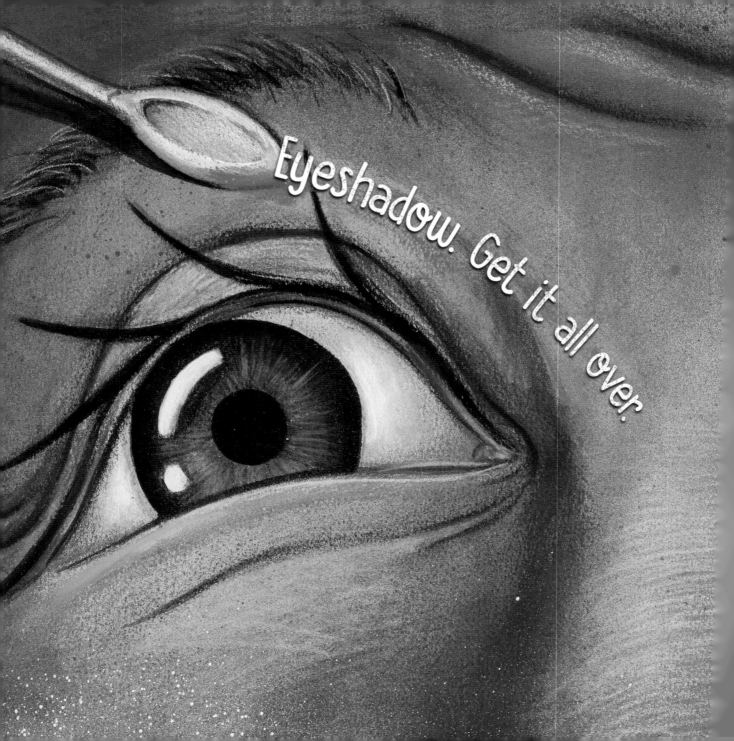

Eyeshadow. Get it all over.

Sombra para los ojos. En todos lados.

Aplica rubor en sus mejillas.

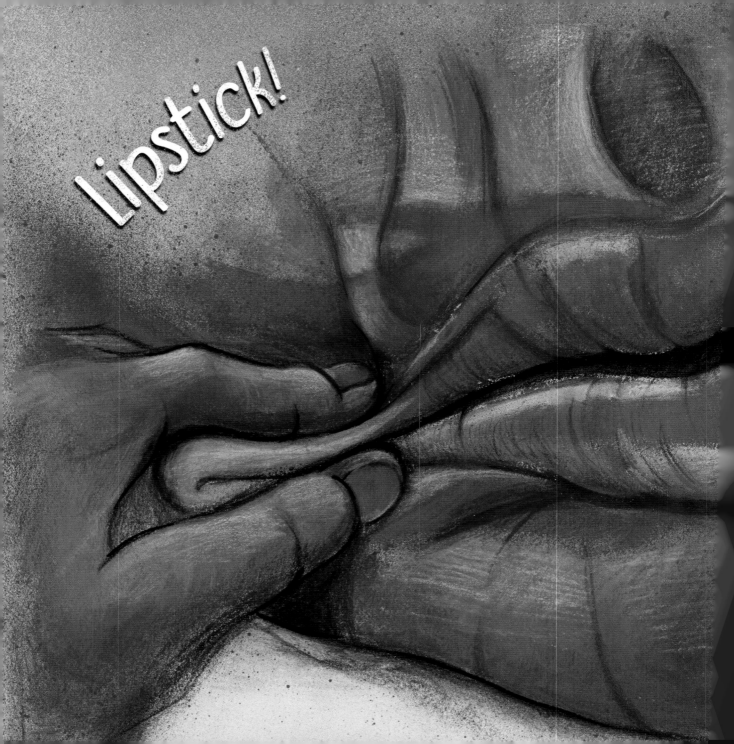

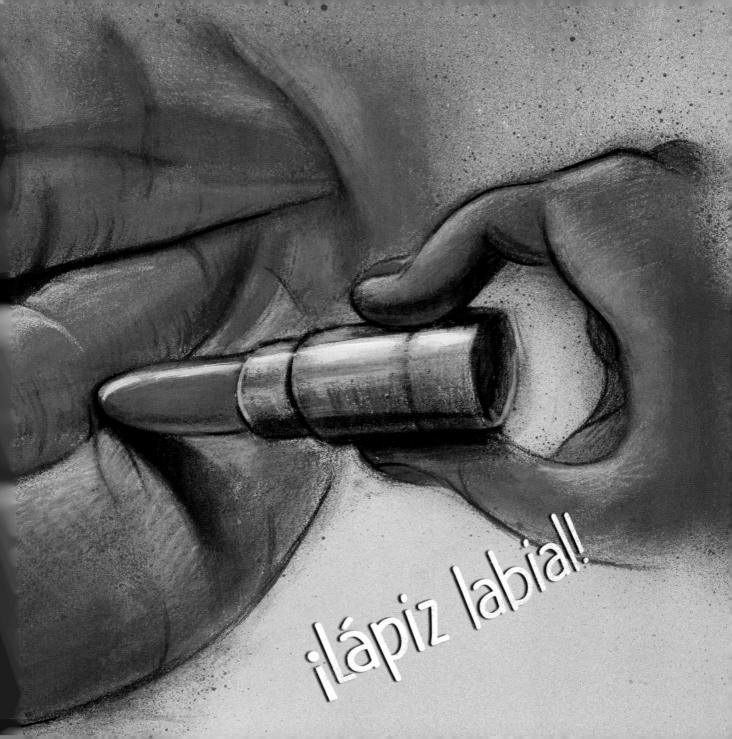

¡Lápiz labial!

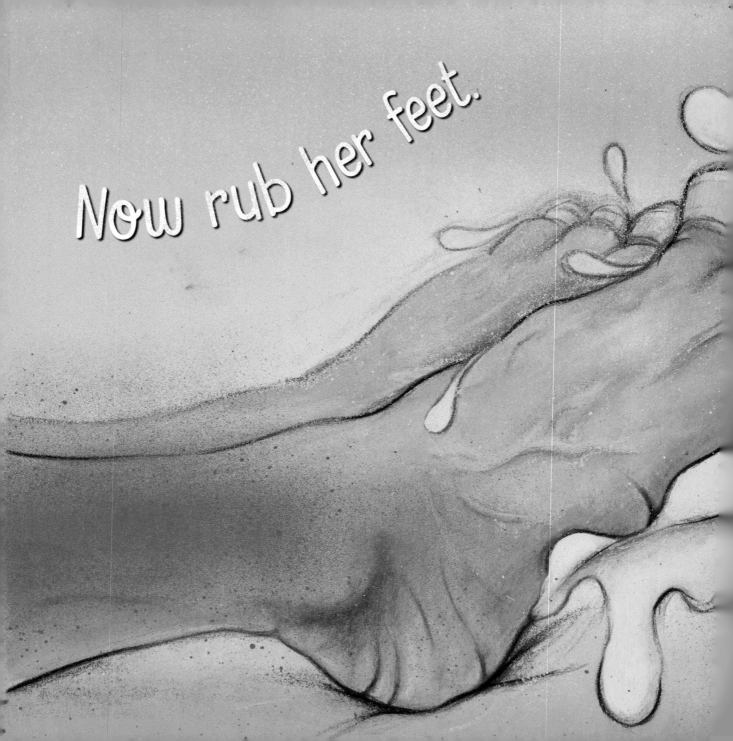

Ahora masaje en sus pies.

Ahora que se levante.
¡Siéntate, Abue!

Put some earrings in her ears.

Pon aretes en sus orejas.

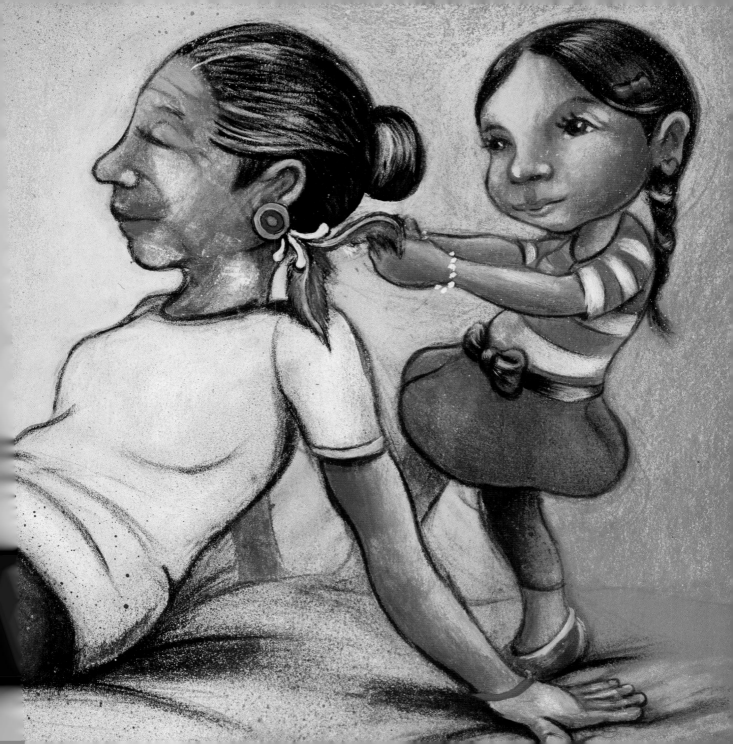

Put a scarf around her head.

Y una bufanda alrededor de su cabeza.

Now I'm done! Aren't you beautiful, Grandma?

¡Ya terminé! ¡Que guapa, Abue!

Who's next? ¿Quién sigue?

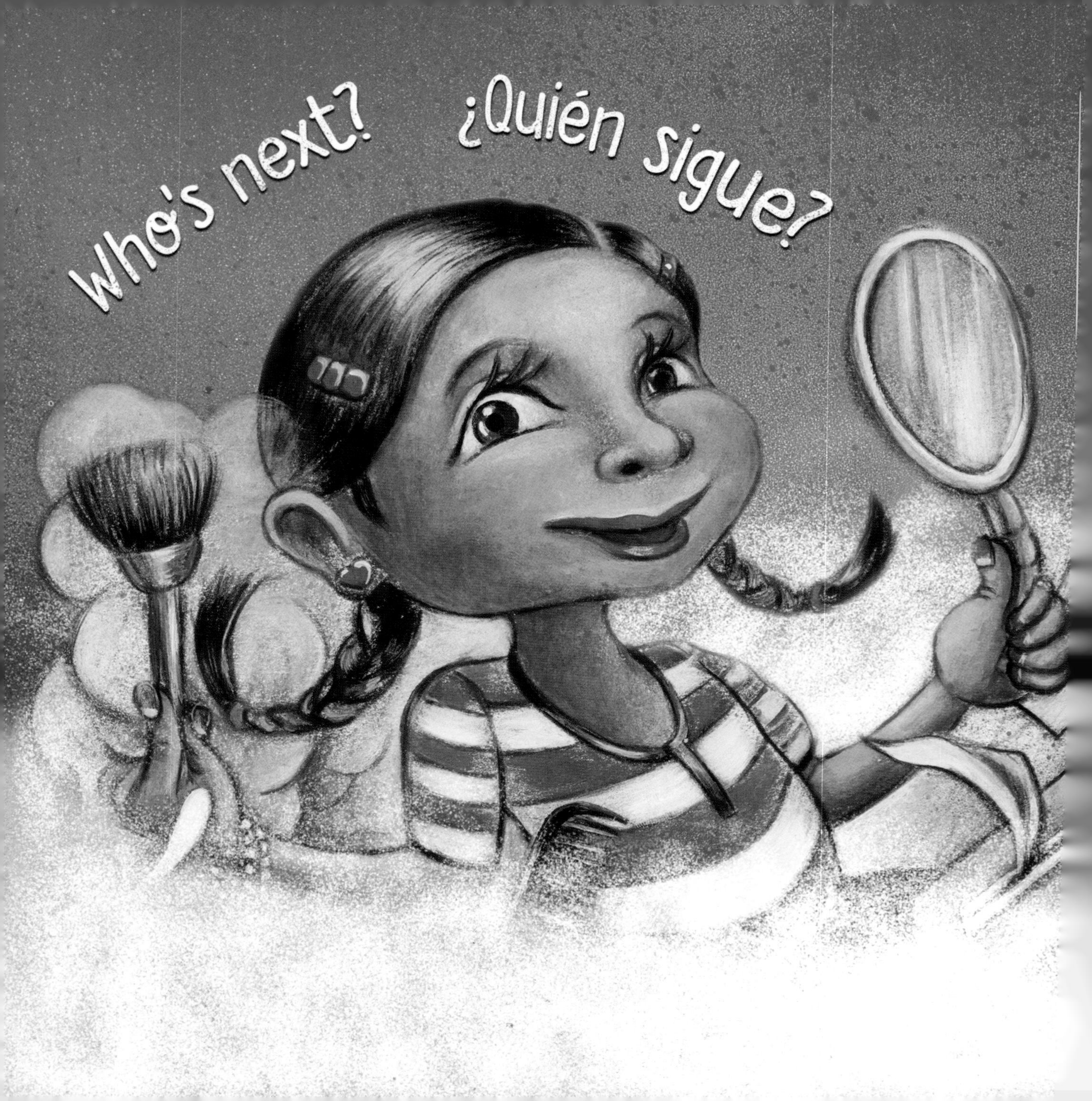